Unexpected Turbulence

KC McCormick Çiftçi

One

L ily Fisher checked one last time to make sure she had everything. Her apartment, her home for the last four years, looked emptier than she could ever remember seeing it, even on that first day when she had moved in.

"Am I making a huge mistake?" she wondered out loud, surveying the familiar landscapes of what had been her home. The kitchen counter had hosted many a late night bonding session with her art school classmates and her fellow interns. The living room, now empty of all the furniture she had found new homes for, had been her favorite place to study, relax, read, eat, and do everything from a yoga session to a full-on potato impression after she had finished her first visual arts internship.

The sound of a horn from the street below got her attention, and Lily checked her watch to confirm the taxi was for her. Her first of three flights, the one taking her from Portland to Los Angeles, was leaving in three hours, and she needed to get this long day underway.

She said one last goodbye to her apartment, leaving her keys on the kitchen counter and the door unlocked behind her, before she closed it behind herself for the last time.

At the airport, there wasn't a single hiccup in the process, as much as Lily might have welcomed one. Still feeling that same sense that this all might be a cosmic mistake that had hit her back in her old home, she would have taken any problems with her luggage or her ticket itself as a sign that maybe she should go back in time and scrap this whole idea.

But her suitcases had been under the maximum weight limit, and because all three of her flights were booked under the same ticket, there were no extra fees for bringing so much luggage on a domestic flight. And even if a small part of her might have enjoyed hearing that she didn't have a seat on the plane, that there had been some mistake and her boarding pass was nowhere to be found, just a few moments after handing over her passport she was holding it again with all three boarding passes tucked securely inside.

Her bags were checked all the way through, and she wouldn't have to see or touch them again until she landed in Wellington and would be grounded for the foreseeable future.

Lily sighed at the thought. Tomorrow—or was it actually going to be the day *after* tomorrow, by the time she landed?—was going to be a new day in a completely new reality. And she was already feeling homesick.

She made herself wait to call her parents until she was through security and had found her way to the gate, stopping to pick up a bottle of water and some snacks first. Lily's family lived in Wisconsin, a fact her mother had been lamenting with extra enthusiasm lately, so much was she wishing that she could have been at the airport to see her youngest child off on this grand adventure of hers.

With a sigh, she dialed the familiar number.

"Hi, Dad." Lily's voice surprised her with how small it sounded escaping her lips.

"Hi, sweetheart," he boomed in response, his smile big enough for both of them. "How are you feeling? Are you at the airport already? It looks like you're going to have great weather in Los Angeles and it's not going to be too different when you get to Sydney, either. I added all the cities you're stopping in to the weather app on my phone, and of course Wellington is there already. I'll be keeping an eye on you."

Unexpected moisture had found its way to Lily's eyes, and she blinked rapidly to clear it, swallowing down a lump in her throat at the same time. "Thanks, Dad," was all she managed in response. She wanted to tell him that she would only be in Los Angeles and Sydney for a few hours each, that the weather wouldn't matter a bit since she wouldn't even be feeling the fresh air on her skin, but all she managed was a small smile. It was his way of showing that he cared, and she knew it would translate to him tracking every hour of her flight path as well.

"Make sure you get some sleep, okay?" she said, forcing some levity into her tone. "You don't need to watch the plane fly over the ocean in real time."

"Well, we'll see about that," he said. "Some nights I don't sleep that well, so if I happen to be awake, then I'll be keeping an eye on you."

"So if I feel like I'm being watched, that's all it is?" Her small laugh was bordering on being genuine now, and she smiled at the image of her dad glued to his phone, refreshing the screen as her plane made its way past Hawaii.

"That's right," he replied, his tone lifting at the end. "Here's your mother, kiddo. She's reaching for the phone. Before I let her take it, though, I just have to tell you how proud I am of you. And that I love you. And also that I'm really looking forward to coming to visit you. I always wanted to go to New Zealand, especially after seeing *Lord of the Rings*, and now I have the best possible reason to visit."

"I love you too, Dad," was all Lily managed before she heard her mother's familiar voice ring down the line.

"Oh, you are such softies," said her mom when she heard Lily's sniffle. "And that's why I love you both. Are you excited? Nervous? Feeling everything all at once?"

"Yes to all of it," said Lily. "I'm not making a huge mistake, am I? Moving so far away? I don't even know anyone in the entire country and it's *so* far away. What if you guys need me? What if something happens, and it takes me a day and a half to get back? This is crazy, isn't it? Am I being irresponsible? A bad daughter?"

"Oh, dear." Her mom's tone had gentled considerably, her voice like a hug from the other end of the phone. "First of all, your father and I would never have let you stay for us. We're both so happy for you and for this adventure you're taking. Heck, he's already looking at tours of Hobbiton on his phone. Yes, Rick, I can see what's on your screen. This opportunity is too good, and it's perfect for you. If I had to push you out of the nest to get you to take it, then that's what I would have done, as much as I do love having you around."

Lily's laugh was watery, unsure of what emotion it was expressing. "It's just so far away, though, Mom."

"Well, yes it is, dear. And that's a problem that neither you nor I can solve. But despite your concerns about us, your dad and I are just fine. Not only do we both take umbrage to any sort of implication that we're getting elderly and infirm and need you as our caregiver, but we *just* retired and taking trips to New Zealand to visit our youngest daughter is exactly the sort of thing we should be doing. We're going to be just fine here, and you're going to have a beautiful life there, and if anything, the distance is going to bring us closer."

"How do you figure that?"

"Well, we'll have to be intentional, won't we? With a time difference like that, we can't very well just pick up the phone on a whim and have a chat. No, we'll have to schedule it and treat it like a sacred appointment because that's what it is." She sighed then. "You'll see, Lily. It's going to be great. What you're feeling right now is normal, and it's not a sign that you're making a mistake. All it means is that you're stepping out of your comfort zone and it's making your ego uncomfortable. That doesn't mean you shouldn't do it. The opposite, actually."

"You're sure about that?" Lily asked, sniffling. "Because I *was* pretty sure this was going to be a great experience, the sort of thing that would make me grow a lot...but today, I'm definitely doubting it."

"Ah, that's the thing, isn't it? I know I always told you to listen to your gut, to your intuition. But just because you have a strong feeling about something, that doesn't mean it's your intuition telling you it isn't the right thing. You've got to differentiate between your gut and your fear. Because being steered by your intuition doesn't mean everything is always going to feel one hundred percent great all the time. You're still going to get scared. So you tell me...is that what this is?"

Lily nodded, her next words coming out almost against her will. "It is. I still want to go, and I know it's for the best, but that doesn't mean I'm not scared it won't work out or sad to be leaving everyone behind."

She could hear her mom sigh, and it sounded like her relief was shared on the other end of the phone line. "That's what I was hoping you would say," her mom said. "We're really proud of you, honey, and all of this is normal. Just keep putting one foot in front of the other, and before you know it, you'll be settled comfortably into your wonderful new Kiwi life."

"And we'll be booking our flights to come visit you!" her dad's voice boomed, from where he was clearly standing right next to her mom. "So remember this conversation when we're the ones calling you to say how nervous we are about the flight."

Lily laughed at that. "You'll be nervous to come on vacation, Dad? I think I can pretty easily talk you out of that just by sending you pretty pictures of Hobbiton."

"That's true," he said. "Not exactly the same as making an international move. You might not know this about me, but I'm a bit of a nervous flyer."

"Really?" Lily blinked rapidly, scanning for memories of her dad on an airplane and coming up empty. On every flight they had taken as a family before, she had either been across the aisle from her dad or so engrossed in a book that she couldn't even conjure up an image of him in that setting. "I had no idea."

"There's no shame in it," her dad said. "It's a pretty natural fear to have, you know, since it's so unnatural for us to be up there in the first—"

"Okay, that's enough," her mom's voice cut in, her dad's voice doing a rapid decrescendo as she increased the distance between them. "Honestly. Does he think he's going to make you less nervous by sharing all the reasons he's scared of flying?"

Lily chuckled at that. "It's okay, Mom. Really. I don't get nervous on planes, and it's definitely not because I haven't thought about it. I just...well, I think it's really cool that we even *get* to fly. That I can get on a couple of planes and end up on the other side of the planet. It would take me a hell of a lot longer to get to Wellington if I had to take a ship."

Her mom groaned. "And if you want to talk about something miserable, we can talk about seasickness."

"I think I'm good, actually." Lily chuckled. "Thank you both for the pick-me-up. I feel a lot better, and I think I'd better wander around and stretch my legs as much as I can before the sitting part of the day starts."

"That sounds great, honey. Just call or text if you need anything. Don't even worry about the time difference. You know we're both going to be sleeping with one eye open until we know you've landed safely on the other side."

"Thanks, Mom. I love you."

"We love you too, Lily. Catch you on the other side."

Lily's first flight of the day went off without a hitch, though the two and a half hours from Portland to Los Angeles were nothing compared to the 15-hour behemoth ahead of her that would see her to Sydney.

After finding the gate, she walked laps from the end of the terminal to her gate and back, noticing a few other passengers who were doing the same.

There were parents with young children and tired eyes, anxious looks on their faces directly dependent on their current efforts paying off and their toddlers sleeping through most of the airtime.

There were couples and individuals, some doing stretches on the carpet and one even lying down with her legs up the wall in a familiar yoga pose. Lily considered for a moment how good it would feel to do just that and then shook her head at the thought of putting her body on the airport carpet. She would have to save legs-up-the-wall pose for tomorrow or the next day, whenever she was settled in her new apartment.

Among the health conscious lap walkers, there also seemed to be a contingent of anxious travelers. With their darting gazes and tapping fingers, Lily thought of her dad and his anxieties about flying as she took in her fellow passengers.

If she was somewhat tempted to approach one of those nervous flyers and reassure him that air travel was statistically the safest way to travel, she managed to restrain herself. The last thing she needed to do now was misread a situation and create fear where it wasn't already thriving. Well, that was the second-to-last thing she needed. The actual last thing she needed was for her comments about safety on the plane to be misconstrued so badly that she found herself on a watch list or missing her flight entirely.

I guess I can just think some positive thoughts in their direction and hope that helps, she considered, using whatever goodwill she could muster to do just that.

When boarding was announced for her flight, Lily felt a flutter of excitement and anticipation. There was no turning back now. A grand adventure awaited her, one that would change her life. How could it not?

Two

As Lily entered the plane, she began counting the rows as she passed them, trying to identify which seat would be hers before she even reached it. Glancing down at the boarding pass in her hand, she saw the same identifier she already knew was waiting for her there: 23H. She groaned softly to herself as it became clear that the "H" referred not to a window or aisle seat as she had hoped, but to a middle seat.

"That's what happens when you don't check in early enough," she muttered under her breath. Pausing at row 20 for a woman to place her carry-on in the overhead compartment, she looked ahead to her future seat, her home for the next 15 hours and felt an involuntary intake of air.

The man seated by the window in row 23 was shockingly handsome. She would have noticed him if she'd seen him at the gate, would have wondered who he was and where he was going and if someone was waiting for him on the other side. She never would have even considered that they might exchange a few words of greeting, much less that he was likely to ask her to move so that he could use the restroom at some point in the next day that they spent sitting together.

She pulled her lips into her mouth, reminding herself to be cool. The specimen of a man that was lying in wait—who had no idea that he was the source of her lack of cool right now—was just a human, just a fellow traveler on his way to the other side of the world. He wouldn't appreciate being ogled any more than she would, and of course, he deserved the politeness of basic human interaction.

As Lily came to a stop in front of row 23, he glanced in her direction and she gave him a small smile before pointing to the seat next to him. "I'm sitting there," she said, immediately wondering why she had felt the need to announce her actions as if he were the owner of the seat, as if she needed to ask him if it were free.

He nodded, gesturing to the seat. "It's all yours," he replied, and she noted with some interest his Australian accent. *Well, Australian or Kiwi,* she thought, reminded once again that she hadn't yet learned to distinguish between the two. *Still, logic bears out that he's from the country where we're going, not the one next door.*

She sidled into her seat, sliding her backpack under the seat in front of her and sighing as she sat up, brushing her hair out of her face. That entire ordeal had been the furthest thing from being smooth or glamorous, two adjectives she was convinced were entirely incompatible with the art of economy flight.

When she glanced to her right, she was equal parts dismayed and relieved that her seat partner's attention had been directed elsewhere, that his eyes were trained out the window as if he were getting paid to inspect the wing from this vantage point. It was comforting that he hadn't witnessed her sideways crab shuffle or the way she had needed all four of her limbs to shove her backpack into its temporary home, but it would have been nice to find him eager to at least exchange a few more words.

Lily folded her hands in her lap, looking around to take in her surroundings for the journey to the other side of the ocean. In front of her, she had her own personal entertainment screen, and on either side were the seats of her fellow passengers. The spot to her left was still empty, but she didn't delude herself into thinking she'd be lucky enough to find it vacant for the whole journey. Her elbows bumped into the armrests, barely leaving her sides, and she willed herself not to feel trapped at the closeness of it all. If there was ever a time *not* to suddenly discover your latent claustrophobia, it was at the beginning of the longest flight you'd ever taken.

"All right?" the man asked, and she turned to find him looking at her with a small, soft smile. He gestured towards the armrest between them. "This is yours," he said, before gesturing to the window. "Window seat gets the window, aisle seat gets the aisle, and the cursed middle seat gets the arm rests as a consolation prize. You should let whoever sits on your other side know that, too."

She nodded, a chuckle escaping her lips. "I probably won't open with that as soon as they sit down, but it's nice to know I've already got someone on my side if it goes to court."

"Oh, absolutely," he said. "It's bad enough, a flight like this, so you've got to find any comfort you can, hey?"

"I guess so," she said, smiling back at him and feeling emboldened to keep the conversation going. "Have you made the trip many times before?"

He shook his head, grimacing at the question. "This is only my second time. I'm not the biggest fan of flying, as it turns out, so I don't expect to make a regular thing out of it."

"Oh?" She raised her eyebrows at him, at his cool demeanor. "You don't have a nervous flyer vibe, but then again, what do I expect that to look like? Sweating bullets and breathing into a paper bag? Those seem like the sort of things you'd do when the plane is actually in the air, not when you're just sitting on the tarmac, thinking about taking off at some point."

He winced again. "Right, well, I can't make any promises about what will happen when we're actually in the air. I'm a fan of keeping an eye on the wing, just reassuring myself that it's still there, but I'm still undecided if that will actually help me keep my cool." He cringed then. "Sorry, stranger. This is definitely the worst way I've tried yet to get to know my seat partner."

"Don't worry about it," she replied. And then, emboldened by his vulnerability, she continued. "If you get scared and need a hand to hold, that's what I'm here for."

"I appreciate the offer," he said, and was it her imagination, or had the tips of his ears turned bright red? "I'm sure that won't be necessary, though."

"Either way, I'm here if you need anything." She held out her hand to him. "My name is Lily, and it seems like if we're going to be stuck together for the next 15 hours, it would be nice to at least have a proper introduction."

"I agree." He reached for her hand, enclosing it in his own. "I'm Ford. Here's hoping for an uneventful journey and a safe arrival on the other side."

By the time they were ready to take off, it seemed like it had been at least an hour since Lily and Ford had interacted. Or maybe that was just the way it felt because part of her so desperately wanted someone to talk to, though even the social mores of air travel seemed unlikely to allow for unloading on a total stranger how much you anticipated missing your family and how uncertain you were of what was waiting on the other side.

True, Ford's flight anxiety might actually make him more willing to act as a stand-in therapist, but that didn't change the fact that Lily was pretty sure she had been raised better than to trauma dump on someone who was stuck in her company for the next 15 hours.

As the pilot pulled away from the gate and began to taxi down the runway, she felt Ford shift beside her. As expected, their third seat companion had arrived, and Lily had felt herself pulled almost magnetically towards Ford by the presence of another man on her other side. It wasn't as if this new man had exuded negative vibes or even tried to use their—*her*—armrest. It simply felt too intimate to be that close to him, while edging closer to Ford felt the opposite.

She was practically leaning on the armrest between them when she heard him suck in a breath as the pilot picked up speed, the airplane just about to lift off the ground.

"You okay?" she breathed, for his ears only.

He nodded, swallowing, and she could see his grip tighten on his knee. "Will be. This is the worst part. Well, this and landing. And any turbulence in between." He let out a chuckle at that, shaking his head. "Pretty much most of the flight, I guess."

Lily reached over and patted his arm, reminding herself to breathe slowly and calmly so that perhaps he could gain some kind of vicarious benefit.

They stayed like that, her close but not close enough to be noteworthy, his breaths somewhat forced but a brave face in place as the plane broke through the gravity that was calling it back to earth, higher and higher until the pilot began to level off.

As the seat belt light turned off with an audible ding, Lily felt the tension relax from Ford beside her.

"We've made it this far," she told him, giving his arm a gentle squeeze before leaning back into her own spot. "Only 14 hours and 50 minutes to go."

Ford winced. "That knowledge doesn't help as much as you might think it does," he said, giving her a smile. "But you're right that we should be happy about the progress we've made." He pursed his lips as he began to dig through the pocket on the seat in front of him. "Now if you'll excuse me, I'm going to try to distract myself with a good book and forget I'm up in the air where humans definitely don't belong."

"You've got it, boss," she said, directing her attention to the entertainment screen. "I think I'll go for a movie myself. Just let me know if you need to get out and use the restroom or stretch your legs or anything like that."

He gave her a silent thumbs up and opened his book, and the two of them slipped into something like comfortable companionship. Lily apologized when her elbow accidentally touched his side, she handed him his drink of choice when the cabin crew made their rounds, and passed his tray back when they were cleaning up. It wasn't much—it wasn't anything, in fact—but it was nice at least to feel like she had an ally on this long journey.

About two hours into the flight, the seat belt sign came on and the captain announced that there was some rough air ahead and a strong likelihood of turbulence, advising everyone to stay in their seats and to keep their belts tightened. Lily glanced at Ford, not wanting to attract attention to what he was likely feeling, and yet seeing it there already written all over his face. He had gone paler and his grip on his book had tightened. His belt had been fastened the whole time, of course, but he checked it then to make sure.

She opted not to say anything in that moment, but just hit the play button of the movie she had paused during the announcement and went back to watching.

A couple of moments later, the turbulence began. At first, it was just a little bit of bouncing, not that different from driving a car a little too fast down a bumpy road.

It was nothing that particularly alarmed her. It was clear, though, that Ford had lost his sense of decorum and was truly feeling the stress of the moment. His hand was now completely gripping the armrest between them, the same one he had told her was hers.

They hit a patch of particularly rough air and it felt like the plane dropped at least a thousand feet in a second. There were shrieks all around them, and Lily even felt her own stomach drop. It wasn't that she normally *enjoyed* turbulence, but it had never bothered her before.

As the plane dropped again, she felt a warm grip on her hand squeezing tightly, and she was grateful for the contact. She turned her hand over underneath Ford's and squeezed back, their fingers locking together through the duration of the turbulence. They didn't say anything to each other, communicating only through the squeezes of their palms.

It seemed as soon as he grabbed her hand, the worst of the drops was over, and she felt herself calming down. But it was clear from the unrelenting strength of his grip that he hadn't exactly chilled out yet.

Even when the plane seemed back to normal, even when the captain had once again turned off the seatbelt sign and the cabin crew had resumed service, his hand was still tight around hers.

She put her other hand on top, his strong hand now sandwiched between hers. "Are you okay, Ford?" she asked, quietly enough not to be heard by their remaining seat companion, who had kept his eyes closed through the entire thing. Whether that was his own approach to facing terror or he genuinely was asleep, she couldn't say.

Ford nodded, but he didn't let go.

She patted his hand. "It's okay," she said. "We're in this together, right? Literally, I mean."

He nodded again, still seemingly having difficulty finding his words.

"Well, I said it to you before," she continued with a smile. "You can hold my hand anytime you want."

In that moment, he seemed to become aware for the first time that his hand was still wrapped around hers. He pulled it back, depositing it in his lap as he tore his eyes away from the window and found hers.

"I apologize," he said, swallowing. "I know you didn't actually mean that literally, and I didn't ever intend to take you up on the offer even if you did." He gestured around them vaguely. "It all just got a little...yeah. That was a bit intense, wasn't it?"

She nodded, tipping her head towards the window. "I'm not normally that bothered by a bit of turbulence, but that one did have me wondering if I shouldn't have made sure my affairs were in order before getting onboard."

He winced. "I know that's a joke, and it's supposed to make me feel better, but—"

"But unsurprisingly, it didn't," she cut in. "Sorry about that. Nothing like a bit of dark humor to try to downplay the fact that we actually got the shit scared out of us." She paused for a beat before continuing. "I am curious, though."

He raised an eyebrow at her. "About?"

She nodded towards the window. "About you choosing to sit by the window, and by the way you had your eyes glued to it while the plane was rocking and rolling. Does it really make you feel better to watch? I think I'd want to close my eyes and think of England or something."

"That's a perfectly valid question." Ford sighed. "And I wouldn't say I like looking out the window in that moment, but it's more like I feel like I have to. I don't know if I think that gives me some amount of control over the situation or what, but somehow it feels like it would only be worse if I weren't paying attention."

"Like the rough air might sneak up on us if you aren't looking for it?"

"Something like that," he said. He tapped on the entertainment screen in front of him, navigating to the page that displayed the flight path before letting out a sigh. "Only 13 hours to go. I can't tell you how eager I am to be safely and happily on the ground again and to not have to do this for as long as I can possibly manage."

"Well, in the meantime, should we try to make the best of it?" At his look of confusion, she continued. "I just mean that maybe a book or a movie isn't really going to cut it in terms of distracting ourselves from our deepest, darkest fears."

"What else did you have in mind?" he asked, his attention fully on her.

Three

"Well, I'm out," said Ford, shaking his head as he handed over his last card, a three of hearts. "You win again."

Lily took the card and immediately began shuffling. "Another round?" she asked, but he was already nodding.

Since the turbulence, she had produced a deck of cards tucked away in her purse, something she had not expected to need. She had brought the cards, a deck she always kept in her purse, because a lifetime as a member of the Fisher family had taught her that you never knew when an occasion might call for cards.

Whether it was her dad playing solitaire on his dashboard while waiting to pick them up from school, or her mom tossing a deck into the backseat, telling her two children to stop bickering and play War already, a game of cards was a daily occurrence at least in their household.

It was tricky, of course, to do much of anything with just those two small trays between them, but Lily and Ford were making it work.

She was glad to see him smiling again—or perhaps for the first time. There was a lightness about him that was the counterpoint of the anxiety she had seen when the flight had gotten bumpy. True, part of her missed the hand-holding aspect of that time, but she knew better than to wish it back. Benefiting from someone else's fear, like cuddling a nervous puppy at the dog park, might feel nice on one level, but it always made her uncomfortable. She'd rather Ford feel safe, comfortable, relaxed, and *choose* to hold her hand in that moment than to see his knuckles turning white as he gripped her fingers and wished to be safely on land again.

"Actually, as much as I'm enjoying this," he said—and she could tell from the upturned nature of the corners of his mouth that he really meant it—"Why don't we take a break and try something different?"

She raised an eyebrow. "What are you thinking?" She nodded towards the window. "I don't think a game of I Spy will be particularly entertaining unless you can manage to spot a whale down there or something."

Ford shook his head. "No, not that. I just thought maybe we could chat more, or, I don't know, play 20 Questions or something, or tell a story?" He shrugged. "I don't have something concrete in mind, but I'd like to talk with you some more, if that's okay with you."

She blinked rapidly. "Of course it is. What about Two Truths and a Lie?"

"That could be a fun." He nodded. "I need a minute to think of mine, or else I'm going to come out with two statements really quickly and then pause so long on the third that you're going to know it's the lie."

"That's fair. Let's take five to think of ours and scramble them up in a surprising order."

"Sounds good." He put his hand to block his tray from her view, like an elementary student trying to keep his test paper a secret from the prying eyes of a classmate. "No cheating."

"You don't have paper or a pen, and I don't have psychic abilities. I think you'll be good." She smiled at him. "Talk to you again in five."

She racked her brain trying to think of the most interesting things about herself, the most unbelievable ones. There was that time when she had broken her nose running into a glass door. There was the fact that she'd never been out of the northern hemisphere.

She knew right away that she didn't want to tell any facts or even a convincing lie that had anything to do with her family because even though she was feeling better, more grounded than she had at the first airport, she wanted to keep that feeling going and not remind herself that her entire family was about to be thousands of miles away.

"Okay, I'm ready," she said, "but you go first."

He shook his head. "All right then. Here goes. I've written three books. I have hobbits in my ancestry and—"

"Don't say 'I hate flying,'" she cut in, "that one will be too obvious."

He chuckled. "I wasn't going to say that, believe it or not. The third and final statement is that I've always wanted to do a shark dive, which sounds crazy, I know."

Lily nodded, pondering. "Right, well it seems obvious that...I mean, I don't want to point out the truth or break some illusion you've been living in…but hobbits aren't real." She pulled a face. "I'm sorry you didn't know that."

He laughed at that. "So that's your guess, is it? That my hobbit ancestry is, in fact, a lie?"

"Yeah, I think it has to be."

"Well then, you'll be disappointed to hear that I've got an aunt on one side and an uncle on the other, who were both hobbits in the *Lord of the Rings* movies." He bit his lower lip. "I bet you feel silly now."

"No way!" She paused to take it all in. "That's so cool. So I guess you've been to New Zealand and visited Hobbiton and all that. I was just talking with my parents about doing that on their trip to come visit me."

Something brightened in his eyes. "You're going to New Zealand too?"

She nodded. "Yeah, one more flight today, not that I want to think about that right now."

"Where to? Auckland? Wellington? Christchurch?"

"Wellington," she said. "I've got a contract there working at the Weta Workshop, at least for the next year. What about you? You didn't answer my question, but I guess the obvious response is that you have, in fact, been to New Zealand."

"Honey, I'm *from* New Zealand. I live in New Zealand. And I'm currently on my way back home to New Zealand. Possibly even on your same flight to Wellington."

"No way," she breathed before pulling her lips into her mouth. "I'm sorry. Maybe I was supposed to know that. It's just I haven't exactly learned to differentiate between Australian and Kiwi accents yet."

He winced. "Well, maybe don't say that to anyone else. But yeah, it's true. I am a Kiwi. Heading home to my beloved Aotearoa and never leaving again."

She tilted her head in confusion.

"That's what it's called in the Māori language. It's good for you to know that. You'll be hearing it a lot."

"Good to know," she replied. "So I guess I still need to figure out what your lie is, huh? Or at this point, since I've already guessed wrong, do you just tell me what it is?"

He gestured for her to continue. "It's not as if we don't have time to prolong the game a bit. What's your next guess?"

Lily paused for a moment, considering. "Honestly, I'm torn right in half. Part of me thinks if you'd written three books you would have already mentioned that, since it's a very interesting fact about yourself. But the other part of me thinks that given your proximity to Australia and the fact that so much of Australian nature seemingly wants to kill us all, you would have to have zero survival instincts to want to do a shark dive." She shivered at the thought. "Haven't you watched *Jaws*? *The Meg*? *Sharknado*?"

He chuckled at that. "Is that the holy trinity of shark films? Because while I'll agree that *Jaws* is absolutely genius, neither *The Meg* nor *Sharknado* feel particularly apt for the discussion at hand."

She waved a dismissive hand. "Doesn't matter. Whether it's a megalodon or a normal sized Great White, thalassophobia is a real thing. I'm so good at it, in fact, at that fear of the deep and the unknown, that if I close my eyes for too long in a bathtub, I can start to freak myself out."

Ford gestured toward the window, the expanse of ocean stretching below them. "So you can't look at that?"

She shook her head. "It's okay from this distance. I just don't want to look at it from close enough that the mysterious creatures in there can *get* me. Not even The Meg could jump high enough to get us up here."

He nodded at that, looking away from the window. "Something new to fear, even all the way up here in the air. Thanks for taking my mind off the turbulence, I guess."

"First of all, it isn't something *new* to fear. Thalassophobia is so innate, I'd guess it's like the oldest fear in the book. And second of all, I believe I distinctly told you that we *don't* have to be afraid of creatures of the deep at 30,000 feet. Not even the kraken has tentacles that long."

He gave the barest hint of a shiver. "Hey, now. If you can be afraid of sharks in the bathtub, I can worry about tentacles and sharp teeth even this far up. Can we agree to be irrationally phobic together?"

"Sure." She gave him a smile. "Lucky for me, there aren't any bathtubs up here." She gestured towards the window shade. "Do you want to close it? Is that better?"

He shook his head. "Not yet. It's somehow comforting, having a bit of daylight. I imagine they'll have us close them when it's time to sleep, or at least when they think it's time for us to sleep. For now, at least, it's a pretty color. Something nice to look at." He swallowed. "Of course, it also feels like it might be the last thing we see before we die, but you know…that's just a perk of flying, I guess?"

Lily exhaled a soft chuckle. "Keeping it real, I see. Okay, back to the game. So does the fact that you seem unbothered by sea creatures mean you *do* want to dive with sharks?"

Ford nodded. "It does." He held up a hand, hurrying to explain. "I'm not saying I want to be in a rickety cage while some overly confident boat captain chums the water to attract the biggest, meanest Great Whites. More like, I'd like to dive with a whale shark, with no concern of being eaten by it. They're amazing creatures, and I think seeing one up close would be just about the coolest thing ever."

"I agree." Off his look, she continued. "Just because I have a healthy fear of things that can kill me, that doesn't mean I don't appreciate the beauty. And also, I *do* understand that shark attacks are a rarity. It's like you said though, irrational. I can tell you every minute from here to Sydney that cars are more dangerous than planes, but is that going to comfort you? Not a chance. It would probably scare the crap out of me, but I'd love to see a whale shark up close. Then again, maybe I'd prefer to see it from a boat rather than in the water."

He smiled at her. "That settles it. On our next trip together, you can sip a piña colada on the boat while I snorkel with the whale sharks."

Lily could feel her cheeks heating, even knowing that he was joking, but she nodded anyway, playing along. "Sounds great. And where exactly will we be doing this? I don't remember Wellington being known for its whale sharks."

"Oh, we have options. We could do Western Australia, Mexico...maybe the Maldives? I'll even let you take your pick for the destination. It *will* be our first vacation together, after all. I can choose the next one."

"Right, sounds good." She blinked a few times, struggling to find her train of thought. "So, that means you aren't a writer? No books under your belt?" She cocked her head to the side. "I have to admit, that's a bit of an odd choice for your lie."

"Yes, but that's what makes it a good lie." He gave her a devastating grin then. "There's a bit of truth in it, as it turns out. That's how I was even able to deliver it in a convincing way."

"What's the truth of it, then?"

"I've written two books," he said, a slightly sheepish bent to his grin. "With any luck, then, that particular lie will be true in the not-too-distant future. Next time I play this little game, I'll have to increase the number again."

"Oh, that *is* good," she said. "I wish I'd thought of that strategy for my own lie. So what kind of books have you written? Anything I may have heard of?" As soon as she asked the question, she winced. "I bet people ask you that all the time, but unless you are secretly Dan Brown or Nora Roberts, the answer is probably no." She reached over and patted his forearm. "Please don't take the fact that I likely haven't heard of your books as a sign that they aren't good enough or renowned enough or whatever. It just means there are too many books in the world for little old me to be aware of all of them."

He placed his hand on top of hers for just a second, a reassuring pat of his own. "Duly noted," he said, "and I can assure you there will be no hard feelings if you aren't familiar with my work. It's unlikely anyway, given that I actually write physics textbooks. Do you, by chance, teach physics?"

She winced slightly. "I wish I did, but I don't. It was one of my better subjects in my senior year of high school, but alas, I ended up working being a VFX artist instead."

"Still, I bet you'd at least appreciate my work. Most of my family and non-work friends just glaze over as soon as I say anything remotely physics-related. It's like I'm speaking a different language. I'll put you on the list to receive an early copy of my next book. Even if you don't read it, you can put it on the shelf and think about the time you reassured its author that he wasn't going to die in a fiery plane crash."

"Ford!" she hissed, dropping her voice. "You can't say the words 'fiery plane crash' on an airplane. It's a major no-no. Like shouting 'fire!' in a theater."

"Sorry." He shrugged. "I can only stop myself for so long before what I'm thinking comes out of my mouth. And it's literally been my mantra since we got on board this death trap."

She sighed. "You, more than anyone, should know how safe we are up here. Surely, when you were studying physics for years and years, you learned about lift? The Wright brothers? Aerodynamics?"

"All of these things and more." He nodded. "But again...phobias are, by definition, irrational. I don't make the rules, but I *am* obligated to follow them." He lifted his chin at her. "So what about you, then? What are your two truths and a lie?"

"Ahh, I thought you'd never ask." She tucked a loose strand of hair behind her ear, playing at preening. "Here we go."

Four

By the time they had finished their game of Two Truths and a Lie, it was like they were old friends. Ford had laughed along with Lily at her story about breaking her nose running into a glass door, he had been appropriately impressed by the movies she'd worked on visual effects for, and he hadn't fallen for her lie about racking up lots of frequent flyer miles, despite her calm demeanor in the air.

They had settled into something that felt comfortable, something that made the hours remaining until they landed seem like they could never be quite long enough. Lily didn't even want to take a nap, was fully prepared to face her first day in the southern hemisphere with no sleep at all, just to keep the fun going.

At one point, when the cabin crew had come around after dimming the cabin lights—"telling us in no uncertain terms it is bedtime," Ford had called it, "like a stern babysitter"—Lily had been aware that she was on the receiving end of a knowing look. The flight attendant had made eye contact with her, darted her gaze to Ford, then looked back at Lily with a smirk that suggested something like approval. As she continued on her way, Lily felt that belly-dropping-out-of-her-body sensation that reminded her she was about to be gossiped about.

She sighed before she could stop herself, earning her a concerned glance from Ford.

"What is it? Something wrong? Did you feel something? Hear something? Just get a strong intuitive feeling that the plane is about to tank into the sea?" He was reaching for the window blind when she stopped him with a soft pat on the knee.

"It isn't that. And you should definitely stop saying things like that, and particularly saying them loudly enough for the people around us to hear," she said, her voice dropped low as she darted a meaningful glance to the seat in front of them, where an older couple were craning their necks as they turned back towards them, peering between the seats.

"Everything's fine," said Ford to the man in front of them. "I'm just a nervous flyer with a terrible sense of humor. It will be in your best interest to ignore me for the remainder of the flight." He turned then to Lily. "So what is it, then? What's with the sighing?"

She shook her head, already embarrassed at what she was about to tell him, yet also confident after the whole Two Truths and a Lie fiasco that she couldn't come up with a lie on the spot to keep him from knowing the truth. "Just the fact that the flight crew is probably gossiping about the two of us right now. I saw it on the flight attendant's face when she sized us up, and it's left me feeling just a bit...exposed here."

He frowned at her. "Why would they be talking about us?" He turned to look over his shoulder. "I don't even see them. How do you know they're talking about us? There are so many people on this flight, and I find it hard to believe that it would be the two of us and only the two of us that would be interesting enough to gossip about. What is there even to say?"

She grimaced. "You're really going to make me say it, aren't you?"

"Say what? I'm completely confused here."

She leaned closer, dropping her voice to a hiss and praying that he wouldn't repeat her words with the same volume that he liked to proclaim the plane was crashing. "Clearly, she thinks something is going on with the two of us. She gave me this look like I've done a good job catching your attention. Which, frankly, is insulting. Not that you aren't a handsome man. Of course you are. It's just that...well, despite my lackluster travel day appearance, I like to think I'm an attractive woman, too. So looking at the two of us with nothing short of shock that a man like you would be wasting his time with a woman like me is, honestly, just wrong. And—"

"That's preposterous," he cut in, and she leaned back so that she could take in his appearance more fully, could try to perceive what had caused his ire before he could even say it. "The idea that you and I are in any way unmatched, I mean. Of course you're a beautiful woman." He shook his head. "That's not what I meant, though. I mean...well, why would they think something is happening here with the two of us?" He widened his eyes then. "I mean...*is* something happening with the two of us?" He held up his hands. "I'll be the first to admit to being a bit clueless with the ladies. Generally, though, I do know when I'm in the middle of something. A flirtation or whatever. I...what *are* we doing here?"

Lily gulped. "I thought we were just being nice travel companions. You know, passing the time and also making sure no one got too nervous during the turbulence."

"That's nice of you to say, to play it off all diplomatically like that. We can both admit, though, that it's only me who was getting too nervous about the turbulence. No need to be so valiant, Lily."

She smiled at him, simultaneously relieved and disappointed by his response. It was good that sharing her suspicions about what the flight attendant thought hadn't made things weird with him. Really, it was. It was just...well, it wouldn't have been *so* bad if he had confidently stated that he did, in fact, have romantic intentions with her and was already planning to ask her out on a date when they were both settled in Wellington.

Don't be ridiculous, she chastised herself. *Any man worth his salt knows not to corner a woman in a situation where she can't escape and ask her out. You should be grateful that has never happened to you, because if it can happen courtesy of the world's most handsome travel companion, it can also happen courtesy of a cab driver or a gynecologist or just about anyone else whose relationship you don't want compromised by personal interest being expressed. Enjoy the flight and let go of the idea that you'll ever see this man again after the plane lands.*

"Hey," said Ford, interrupted her thoughts, the reverse pep talk she was giving herself. "I just remembered that we might be on the same flight to Wellington. Do you know what time yours leaves?"

Lily pursed her lips. "Let me check. My brain is turning into mush this far into the travel day, so all the times and gates I had memorized once upon a time are long gone now. Ancient history." She scrolled through the flight confirmations saved on her phone, finding just the right one. "It leaves at four. About two hours after we land, I guess." She blinked. "I'm surprised I booked it with that short of a layover. Normally I'm so nervous about one flight getting delayed and it messing up all the subsequent ones, and yet here I am booking a two-hour layover between two international flights."

He chuckled. "You'll be fine. It's not as if you'll have to enter Australia, since your bags are checked through and you already have your boarding pass. You'll just do the whole international transit thing, and it should be a piece of cake." He was already checking his phone, a smile slowly spreading across his face. "Unbelievable!" he said finally. "We're on the same flight. That's awesome." The grin he gave her then was so earnest, so sincere, and so broad, that she had to look away.

So much for resigning herself to the idea of never seeing him again.

"I'll bet if we ask nicely at the gate, they'll even let the two of us sit together again," he said. "If you want that, of course, I mean. Not trying to force my company on you."

"Oh," she said, her next words not coming easily, her brain working as if it were frozen.

"It's okay," he began. "It was just an idea, but I'm sure you will have had enough babysitting me and my flight anxieties by the time we get to Sydney. We can just go our separate ways, and if we happen to bump into each other at the gate, we can just nod and go on with our lives. Heck, we can do the same thing if we bump into each other in Wellington. Or we can just not even acknowledge each other if that's what you prefer. I was going to say, you might like to have a friend in the city, but you don't even have to have a friend at the airport if that isn't what you want."

"Ford," she said, silencing him with a hand on his arm. "I wasn't trying to think of a way to let you down gently. The reality is, of course, I would love to sit with you on the next flight. I was just...well, to be honest, I was surprised that *you* would even want that."

He frowned. "Why wouldn't I want that?"

She shrugged. "There's no special reason, really. I just figured...well, people have nice interactions on planes all the time, but when does that ever turn into something more? Even a friendship, I mean," she rushed to explain, not wanting to imply again that there could or should be something romantic blossoming between them. "People generally *do* go their separate ways, and there is nothing wrong with that."

"That's true," he said. "Most of the time, anyway. One of my friends from uni, actually, he's from England, but he studied in Wellington for a year and that's when we met. He met his partner on an airplane. The two of them kept seeing each other around, finally struck up a conversation, and they've pretty much been inseparable ever since. So it does happen."

Lily nodded, something rising from her subconscious as she took in his words. "You're right. I think one of my brother's friends had something similar happen. Not that they kept seeing each other, but that there was one long flight back to the US from Korea, I believe, and the two of them pretended to be a couple to get this annoying guy to leave her alone." She shrugged. "Last I heard, they were still together."

"So it seems like your argument does not hold water."

"I can't even prove my own point," she said with a laugh, "so there is no reason at all for me to refuse to be your travel buddy on the next flight. Is there anything cool we can do in the Sydney airport to pass the time?"

He grinned at that, as if he were so happy by the idea of getting to spend more time together that he was already planning their every minute. "Oh yes, lots," he said. "There's this great long walk we'll get to do from one terminal to the other, and we'll probably have to go through security again. Shouldn't have to do passport control, if I'm remembering correctly. And then, well...if you like duty-free shopping, you're in luck because there will be plenty of that. But if you're looking for, I don't know, a quick trip to the Sydney Aquarium or the Harbor Bridge, I'm afraid you're going to need more time to do that."

"We can do that on our next vacation," she said before she could think better of it. "The one after the whale sharks, I mean."

"I'll add it to the list," he said, a nod of utter seriousness. "We'd better start saving our money because it looks like the two of us have a lot of traveling to do together."

"Hmm," was all she could say, the only way she could keep from being consumed by the frustration and confusion of knowing how much of this was a joke and how much of it was the fodder for something real to flourish. Oh, she knew the two of them weren't traveling to see whale sharks anytime soon. But meeting up for coffee in Wellington seemed well within the bounds of reality for their shared future. Ford might even introduce her to some of his friends, help her start making some local connections. They might have dinner together and if Christmas rolled around, and she wasn't going to be able to go home to see her family, he might invite her to come spend it with his...

Okay, now you've gone too far again. Back it up, Fisher, she chided herself. *This has gotten entirely out of hand.*

It was hard *not* to let it get out of hand, though. This taste of life with Ford that she was getting on the plane was too good not to want more. He was easy to be around, so much fun to laugh and joke with, and in this enclosed space, she had his nearly undivided attention. It was an addictive reality to visit, especially for 13 hours straight, and she was already hooked on imagining that it could be her reality for far longer than that if things went right. It was impossible not to want it.

The fact that it was going to continue, that the two of them would be strolling through the Sydney Airport in a way that probably looked identical to countless couples doing the same thing, was amazing and stress-inducing in equal proportions. Of course it sounded like fun to let the illusion continue. It also meant that by the time they landed in Wellington together, it was entirely possible that she would expect to walk out of the airport hand-in-hand, the two of them driving in companionable, sleepy silence back to the home they shared with their 2.5 children, dog, and white picket fence.

"I'm going to be really homesick in Wellington," she blurted, immediately feeling a blush rise to her cheeks at the vulnerability of her declaration. "I've never been this far away from my family, and I already cried once at the airport today when I talked to my parents. I'm not sure how it's going to go, if I'm going to be able to do it."

To her pleasant surprise, Ford gave her a knowing nod and a reassuring smile. "That friend of mine I told you about, Guy? It was hard for him, too, being so far away from everyone back home. Now that he's back in England, though, he misses the rest of us still in Wellington, probably almost as much as he missed his family then. It's just the unfortunate reality of this massive planet of ours, that if you travel and meet people around the world, you're going to love them, and you're always going to be missing someone. It's the beauty of it, but it's the curse of it, too."

"Oh gosh, I didn't even think about that," said Lily. "I think I told you about being homesick just to explain why I might get a little too attached to you a little too quickly. I mean, it's not like I know anyone in Wellington yet, other than the woman that hired me. But I didn't even consider that, if you and I become good friends or something, when my contract ends and I decide to go back home to Wisconsin, I'd end up missing you as much as I miss my family." Her cheeks were burning even brighter now, she was sure of it. "I mean, that would be true of whoever

I become friends with in Wellington. I'm not expecting anything from you."

"You should," he said, a new cheekiness in his grin. "We've got all these hypothetical trips planned for the future already, so you'd better expect something from me. Sounds like an unfair division of labor if you don't." He leaned closer then, the playfulness dropping from his face. "But really, though, I will gladly be your first Wellington friend. A flight like this is a bit of a bonding experience, you know? You were there for me, literally held my hand when I needed it, and I'm going to what...abandon you when you're on your own in a new city, a new country? Nah, that's not how my parents raised me. I'll look after you, Lily." He flung an arm around her shoulder, pulling her closer despite the armrest between them. "You're going to be just fine."

She sniffled then, surprised by the cocktail of emotions she was feeling. It was nice to have a friend, but it was an alarming reality check to consider that this adventure she had so happily rushed off to was likely the reason her heart would be split in half for the rest of her life. If she decided, by some strange twist of fate, to settle in New Zealand, she would always miss home. If she moved back home at the end of her contract, she already knew, even without yet setting foot there, that she was going to miss New Zealand. That she would wonder what the *Sliding Doors* version of herself who stayed there was doing, every minute of every day.

"I hope so," she said, blinking watery eyes at him. "I really do."

Five

"Of course you're going to love it there," he said, nodding fervently like the movement of his head was going to drive hers up and down too, was going to convince her by the mere power of suggestion that she agreed with him. "And I didn't mean to make it worse by suggesting that no matter where you are, you're always going to miss someone. Let's just focus for right now on the fact that you miss your family. And maybe the best way to focus on that particular ailment is to think about all the fun things waiting for you in Wellington."

"I'm listening," she said, smiling through the emotion she was feeling. "I could use some suggestions. I'm looking forward to getting started with my job, of course, but it probably won't be the best for my adjustment phase there if I just spend every spare minute thinking about work. Friends and hobbies might be a good idea."

"Right. What sort of things do you like to do? Hiking? Shopping? Water sports? Museum hopping?"

"Hiking sounds like the best option there," she said. "I'd love to do some exploring, maybe take some weekend trips around the North Island and when I get a break from work, head down to the South Island."

Ford was already nodding. "These are great ideas, Lily. And in fact, if I may be so bold, I'm going to suggest that we move the weekend North Island trips to the very top of our 'trips to take together' list and also move them from the hypothetical to the reality. We could go up to Auckland for a couple days, maybe Napier another time. The Coromandel Peninsula is definitely worth a visit. And we can't forget all the various *Lord of the Rings*-related sites, of course."

"Really? You would do that for me?"

He shook his head. "I would do that *with* you. It's a beautiful country, my homeland. And I'm ashamed to admit that I don't spend nearly enough time appreciating it. Having the excuse of showing you around would give me just the right opportunity to remedy that. Unless, of course, you don't want that. If you'd rather go on your own, I completely understand and I could help you fig-ure that out, too. Car hires, hostels, things like that." He wasn't quite meeting her eyes now.

"No, no," she interjected, almost too forcefully. "I would love to have you as my travel buddy. It's just...well, this is a bit awkward to ask."

He nodded. "Go ahead. It's just the two of us here, and I promise not to laugh."

She gave him a small smile. "Well, I'm just wondering if there's someone special waiting for you at home who might not be too keen on you spending so much time out there in the world with a single woman."

He barked out a laugh. "Oh, that's an important question indeed! Well, rest assured, if I were married or in a relationship, I wouldn't be dumping my partner weekend after weekend to spend those days with you." He smiled at her then, shaking his head. "No girlfriend, no wife, no one I'm seeing casually who thinks we're a couple, no kids. I *do* have a cat waiting for me at home that my sister is currently feeding, but he shouldn't be a problem. Ollie is a bit of an adventure cat, so he'll probably want to tag along on at least a couple of those trips. For the ones he can't, that's what June is for. June is my sister, and Ollie's favorite cat sitter."

"Really?" Lily frowned as she studied Ford's face, looking for any hint that he was joking. "You would really do this? You aren't joking? Or just being nice because I got a little emotional on an airplane?"

He shook his head. "Were you just being nice any of the times you tried to reassure me that—" He leaned even closer and dropped his voice to a whisper, finally learning his lesson. "—we weren't going to die in a plane crash? No, I don't think you were. I think you wanted me to feel better and probably you also wanted to reassure anyone within listening range that my fears were ungrounded. So the point is, then, that both you and I benefited from that particular kindness of yours. And both you and I will also benefit from me taking you on some weekend adventures around my homeland."

"It just seems like one of those kindnesses is a lot larger than the other."

He nodded. "I agree. If you hadn't reassured me that today is not the last day of my life, then I might have had some kind of medical emergency that forced the pilot to turn the plane around. Repeat that experience a time or two, and I'm not sure I'd ever have actually been able to make the journey home. I'd have to set up a new life in America, and quite frankly, I am just not prepared to do that." He smiled at her then. "I'm not as brave as you, Lily, it seems. Neither about the air travel nor about starting over in a new country."

"Well, we'll see how brave this move of mine is after I'm either able to settle in and enjoy my new life or I crash and burn and have to go back home with my tail between my legs."

He winced. "Not that I'm not a fan of mixed metaphors, Lily, but if you could refrain from using the phrase 'crash and burn' until...oh, let's say *tomorrow* to be safe, that would be truly appreciated."

She pulled a face. "Sorry about that. Poor choice of words. I promise I wasn't trying to remind you of where we are, in relation to the earth, I mean."

"Not at all." He shook his head. "Actually, let's talk about literally anything else. You were saying that the result of this move of yours is going to determine whether it was brave or not, yeah? Something to that effect?"

Lily nodded. "Right. It will turn out to have been a brave move if it's this great experience, right? If it moves my career forward or ends up facilitating me meeting my future husband or unlocks some other opportunity I can't even fathom right now. But if it turns out that I'm miserable or that I got tricked into working for a shady company or everything falls apart right in front of my eyes...well, how could I still claim that was a brave move? It would seem, on that occasion, at least, that it was actually a colossally stupid move instead. That if I had just stayed put, everything would have been better, but I had to go all the way to the other side of the world just to have my life fall apart."

Ford's hand landed on top of hers, and she looked up to find his warm brown eyes searching her face. "With all due respect, Lily, I couldn't possibly disagree more."

She raised her eyebrows. "Oh? Well, enlighten me, please."

He kept his hand right where it was, his fingers tapping gently on the back of her hand as he spoke, splitting her attention between what he was saying and the sensation of his skin on hers.

"No matter what happens, it's brave to take a risk. And no matter what happens, there's no way of knowing that things would have been different or better if you'd made the other choice. Think about it. Unless you have a twin back home as a control variable, there's no real experiment happening here. You're the only one of you there is—unless, of course, we start talking about the multiverse—and time only flows in one direction, so there's just no way of running a scientifically sound experiment to see what choice is the best. Which choice produces the desired result? I, for one, am sure that this is the best choice you could have made in this moment. It doesn't matter if there's a better one, if you would have unlocked different opportunities if you'd gone to Scotland or Tunisia instead. You made a choice, the simple fact of which making a choice and acting on it is something that holds so many of us back for so long, and now you're following through on it. That's brave and I can guarantee you I won't change my mind on this one."

She smiled at him, but a frown creased her forehead at the same time. "What makes you so sure that this is the best choice?" She exhaled a small chuckle. "Is it just hometown pride? It would be disloyal of you as a Kiwi to think there could possibly be anywhere else in the world that's better?"

He squeezed her hand then, the pressure drawing her eyes, then following the line of his arm up to his face, where she found his gaze intent on her. "I know it's the best choice because it's the reason you're here and we're talking. There are infinite other things you could be doing in this moment, and yet I, for one, am immeasurably grateful that this is where you find yourself."

Lily was dumbfounded, her mind a swirling mass of colors and shapes as she tried to find the right words to say. The right way to check if he was saying what she thought he was saying, the right way to tell him that she felt that same way, the right way to create a moment that would replay in her mind for years to come. *The right story to tell our grandkids one day*, a voice chimed in from the back of her mind.

As she opened her mouth, prepared in no way, shape, or form to speak with eloquence and wit, they were hit with another bout of turbulence, the plane dropping drastically as the surrounding passengers, once asleep, awoke with shrieks. The same sound escaped from Lily's lips, her grip on Ford's hand tightening as she watched the color drain from his face.

Ding! The sound echoed throughout the plane as the seatbelt sign once again illuminated, the flight attendants moving with increased speed towards their own seats.

"Ladies and gentlemen, this is your captain speaking. Please stay in your seats with your seatbelts securely fastened. We've got another bit of rough air ahead of us, and we will be experiencing some more turbulence. Again, please remain seated with your seatbelts fastened until we turn off the seatbelt sign."

"Are you okay?" Ford asked, his eyes searching her face like there was something written there, a clue as to her wellbeing.

She nodded, gulping for air. "Are you? That one came out of nowhere." She placed her other hand on top of his, and he did the same, all four of their hands clasped together on the armrest.

"I am," he said, his smile forced as the plane dropped again. "Let's just hope we get to the other side of this soon."

"Yeah," she said, taking a few deep breaths. "I have to say, I think I'm starting to understand why flying makes you so nervous."

He forced a laugh. "Don't say that. If you start down that road, then all hope is effectively lost for me in terms of keeping my shit together." He swallowed, eyes darting. "Now is maybe not the best time to tell you that our final destination is affectionately known as Windy Wellington, which means sometimes taking off and landing there can be just a bit...exciting."

"Oh good," she said, sarcasm dripping from her words. "I was afraid this was all going to be behind us way too soon." She continued to breathe deeply as the bumps and dips grew smaller, the pilot seemingly getting them safely to the other side of the rough air.

"You're really okay?" she asked Ford again, squeezing his hands in hers. "I wasn't exactly there to comfort you when that all happened." She let out a self-deprecating chuckle. "Seems like I was too busy shrieking myself to pay much attention to what was going on with you."

"I think that's why I handled it better this time," he replied, squeezing her hands back. "You were in distress, and I just wanted to make sure you were okay. It's sort of the opposite of the whole 'put on your own oxygen mask first' idea, I guess. I didn't even have a chance to ask myself if I was okay, because it seemed pretty clear that you weren't."

"That's sweet." She extracted one of her hands from their cuddle puddle, using it to tap lightly on his chest. "And I sincerely appreciate the comfort. However, I have to beg you *not* to disregard the instructions should any oxygen masks appear. No matter how much I shriek or holler, yours has to go on first."

He gritted his teeth. "Let us *sincerely* hope that no oxygen masks drop down during this flight." Ford shook his head. "It's like getting stressed about one little bump on the flight caused some kind of *Freaky Friday* moment and now you're the one making inappropriate jokes about our safety. Next thing I know, you're going to start joking about crashing and—"

She moved her hand up from his chest to cover his lips, ever so slightly too late to keep the too-loud words from coming out of his mouth. Once her fingers touched his lips, though, the mood between them changed, from something playful and light-hearted to something electric, something so full of potential and energy that she immediately tried to pull her hand away, like she had touched a stove burner only to find it was still hot.

Her movement was to no avail, though, because Ford had captured her wrist, his hand holding hers in place just a moment longer before he moved her palm to his cheek, his eyes closing for the barest of flashes before he released both of her hands, his own coming to rest in his lap.

"What are we doing here?" she asked him, the words escaping before she could think better of it. Perhaps it was the illusion of a near-death experience—because yes, a few minutes out from that little turbulence scare, she could see it for what it was and knew she had been in no real danger—but there was a part of her that didn't care how awkward it might make things between them. She wanted to know what was going on, if she was misreading a friendly interaction as flirtation and promise, or if there really was a tangible presence here with them, pulling each of them toward the other.

If Ford had praised her once for her bravery and risk-taking, let him do it again now. If not, let him criticize her for it. Either way, she needed to know where they stood.

Six

F ord's sigh was so deep the couple in front of them started glancing back again, and Lily held a finger up to her lips to silence him, stifling her own laugh at the same time.

"That bad, huh?" she whispered. "Forget I asked."

"I just wish I had a better answer for you," he said, "because I don't have a clue." He touched his hair, swiping it off his forehead. "But if it's feeling to you like there's something there, then you're not crazy. I feel it too, but I just don't know what it *is*."

"What do you mean?"

"Well, is it the connection of comforting each other through a stressful situation? Because that does make sense. Endorphins and oxytocin and all that good stuff."

"Oh, right," she said, feeling herself deflate at the thought. Of course there was a perfectly rational explanation for what they were feeling. She should have thought of that before she opened her mouth and inserted her foot. "That makes sense," she said, not meeting his eyes.

"Hey." His hand was on her arm, drawing her attention back to him. "I'm not saying that's what it is. What do I know? I'm a physicist, not a psychologist. I'm just not exactly a mystic when it comes to things like love and fate and all that, no matter what happened to my friend and your friend and all the other many people who I'm sure met their soulmates on airplanes."

"That makes sense," she said again, kicking herself for not having a different reply ready to go.

"I just think we need to give it more time," he said then, surprising her. "Because it's undeniable. There *is* something there. But we aren't going to know what it is until we spend some more time together." He let out a mock sigh then, deep and long. "It looks like now we definitely have to take those weekend trips together. For science."

She rolled her eyes at him. "For science."

He gave her hand a squeeze, nodding towards the screens in front of them. "How about a movie for our first date, then?"

"First date?" Her eyes were wide, she knew, and she made no effort to hide her shock. "You're already talking about first dates over here?"

"There's no better time than the present to get an experiment underway. Now that we know the two of us can support each other in times of emotional duress and also that we can find something to laugh about, some way to entertain ourselves and while away the hours, we face the ultimate test."

"Choosing a movie?" she guessed.

He nodded. "Exactly. With all the options on board, can we find something we both enjoy? A quest like this, well, it can make or break a potential couple, Lily. I won't lie, I've seen pairings brought down by less. The mission is difficult, but should you choose to accept it, there just might be beautiful things in store for us." He shrugged. "Of course, should you choose not to accept the mission, this message will self destruct—"

Her hand was over his mouth again, her chest quaking with silent laughter. "You can't keep joking about things blowing up."

"Maybe," he breathed, his lips suddenly at the shell of her ear, "I do these things just to keep you close. Had you considered that possibility?"

She shook her head as she pulled back, all mirth gone from her expression. "Really?"

He shrugged. "That time, definitely. After you clapped a hand over my mouth, I was a goner. I would have said just about anything to get you to do it again."

"You're ridiculous." She chuckled, shaking her head at him. "So you have a real thing for women shushing you? Touching your lips?"

"Apparently." He gave her a cheeky smile. "I'm as surprised as you are. This has never been a particularly compelling interest of mine, and yet today it's just about all I can think about."

"Right." She gave him a single nod before directing her attention back to the entertainment system. "We need to find a movie before you get yourself in trouble." She pointed him towards his own screen. "And you need to look, too. This isn't some kind of test where you make me look for the perfect movie and then judge my selection. Your taste is on the line, too."

"Of course," he said, already scrolling through the cat-alog of entertainment options. "I wouldn't dream of putting you on the spot like that."

They were silent for a few minutes, each of them focused on the screen in front of them. Lily made note of the new releases she had been meaning to watch, alongside a selec-tion of old favorites, from buddy comedies and timeless love stories to some of the action-adventure movies she had watched on replay as a child.

"Probably not a new release, right?" she asked. "I mean, if neither of us has seen it, how can we know if it's any good?"

"Couldn't agree more," he said. "There's nothing worse than starting a movie with high expectations and then forcing yourself to finish it even though it's literal dog water."

Lily shook her head. "No way. In that instance, the only correct path forward is to abort the mission. You don't have to finish a movie just because you started it. Same is true for a book."

He darted a glance at her long enough for her to see his raised eyebrow. "Maybe you can do that, but I find my-self stuck, sitting through terrible dialogue or the biggest of plot holes simply because I, the eternal optimist, keep hoping it's going to get better."

"Well, we can agree to disagree on that," she said. "When that inevitably happens on one of our weekends away to-gether, I'll just go to bed while you stay up finishing your terrible movie."

She froze in place as soon as she'd finished her sentence, counting all the ways her words had applied pressure, had suggested the deepening of things between them. Sure, they had already talked about taking weekend trips together. But she had brought it to a new level with the talk of what would happen during the *nights* on those trips. Would they be sharing a hotel room? When she retired early to that bed, would it be the same one Ford would be sleeping in? And would that have been the plan all along, or would it be something that was only happening because their hotel had mistakenly booked them a room with the trope of all tropes, only one bed?

But Ford didn't bat an eye. "Glad to have that figured out in advance. For now, though, no new releases. Nothing you haven't already seen and loved."

Lily exhaled slowly, trying to keep herself from audibly sighing with relief. It felt like she had dodged the bullet of all bullets, a major conversational faux pas. "Good plan. And perhaps err on the side of caution if it was something you watched and loved when you were, say, 12 years old. How many times have I revisited a childhood fave only to find out it hasn't exactly aged well...or else my tastes have changed to the point of being unrecognizable?"

"That's true, too," he said, still scrolling. "Though there certainly are the ones that stand the test of time." A few more seconds of silence as they both took in their options. And then...

"Ooh, *Jurassic Park*," he exclaimed at just the same moment her finger came to rest on the entire collection of Jurassic films. "How does that sound?"

Lily was nodding. "Definitely one of my favorites as a kid, and...yeah, it holds up. I can watch that movie just about any day and never get tired of it."

"Same here," he agreed, a large smile on his face. "And here I was afraid we were going to have to watch a movie about a plane crashing or something like that."

"Ford!" she shrieked, launching herself at him to stop the words coming out of his mouth, too late this time. Whether it was his statement or, more likely, her own exclamation, they found themselves on the receiving end of several stern glances. "Sorry!" she whisper shouted, ducking her head as her cheeks burned. "Sorry! Won't happen again."

Ford lifted the armrest between them and pulled her close to his side, queuing up the movie on both screens as he made a tsking sound into her ear. "I think I'll just keep you right here by me so you don't have to do something like that again," he said. "For the safety of our fellow passengers, I mean."

She shook her head at him. "You could also consider *not* making inappropriate comments about our safety. That would put the whole thing to rest, too, wouldn't it?"

"Hmm, an interesting hypothesis," he said, handing her a set of headphones. "Maybe we can try it your way another time. For right now, at least, it's probably safest if I just keep you close."

She couldn't bring herself to protest it, to try to convince him that *he* was the one who needed to behave, when it felt so good, so right, as natural as a cat in a cardboard box to snuggle right into his side. She offered up her silent gratitude at all the unexpected turns this day had taken, all the decisions and variables that had led her to be right here, close enough to Ford to feel his chest rise with every breath.

"Ready?" he asked. When she nodded, he hit play on both of their screens and settled back, one arm around her shoulders. She let out a sigh, willing the moment to last for as long as it possibly could.

The remainder of the flight was surprisingly smooth, given the bumpy nature they had become accustomed to in its first half. There had been no more occasion for grasped hands, for whispers of comfort. And yet Lily and Ford had remained closer to each other than they had been in any of those stressful moments, the armrest between them a long-lost memory and nothing more.

After they had enjoyed *Jurassic Park,* pointing out all the most iconic scenes and delivering whispered renditions of their favorite lines, they had each chosen their own movies, both losing themselves in a new release at the top of their to-be-watched lists.

It was an unusual sensation, Lily thought, to be so physically close to someone and be engaged in distinct activities. As she chuckled along with the comedy she had chosen, she briefly wondered if Ford was enjoying his science fiction selection or if he was merely forcing himself to finish what he had started. She smiled at the thought, amazed that despite knowing him for such a short time, his foibles were already like old, familiar friends to her.

When their movies ended, within fifteen minutes of each other, the cabin crew made an announcement about the flight's final meal service happening shortly. Lily looked at Ford with expectation, the flight path map already open on the screen in front of him.

"About two hours to go," he told her in a soft voice. "So we'll eat, they'll clean up, and before you know it, it'll be time to land." He shook his head. "I just can't get over how much better this flight is than the one I took to California two weeks ago."

She shook her head, mimicking him. "Amazing, isn't it? And what do you think the difference is?"

He elbowed her in the ribs. "Beats me," he teased. "Probably something to do with the in-flight menu, if I had to guess. They served fish on the last flight, and if that isn't the harbinger of doom, then I don't know what is."

Lily recoiled, looking at him askance. "I know you're kidding, but that is truly awful. I don't know what it is about eggs and fish on airplanes, but I've never had an experience with either one that didn't make me wish I'd ordered the vegan menu."

"Then here's hoping our final meal in the air doesn't contain either," he said, lifting his arm and nodding for her to return to her position there.

Instead, Lily replaced the armrest. "They're going to be telling us to put these things down soon enough, anyway, and I really don't need any more judgmental side eye from flight attendants today." She lowered her voice even quieter. "Obviously they all know we didn't board this flight together, and the fact that we're this cozied up now is going to be the kind of story they'll hear about in even the remotest locations."

"The small team of scientists currently on Antarctica will be talking about it any minute now."

She nodded. "The astronauts at the international space station, too. It will be their hot lunchtime gossip." She frowned. "Of course, I don't even know what time it is *here*, so I don't know how I could be expected to know which meal they're eating in space."

Ford checked his watch. "Well, this is still set to California time, but unfortunately I can't tell if it's AM or PM. All I can say for sure is that you and I have both been up for entirely too long, and we're bound to start getting loopy sometime soon."

"Oh, sometime soon that's going to happen? So every ridiculous thing that's happened in the last 11 hours is...what...just our innate senses of humor?"

He gave her an affirmative nod. "If the joke generated actual laughs, then I take total credit for it. If it was an embarrassment, then that's the sleep deprivation talking. That's my entire system."

"Seems simple enough. I might give it a try."

A flight attendant materialized next to them soon after that, serving a light breakfast, which they ate while continuing to chat. Lily shared her blueberry muffin with Ford, and he gave his grapes to her in return.

When it was time to pass their trays back for collection, the man seated on Lily's other side took the opportunity to engage them for the first time on the flight.

"Where are yous headed?" he asked, his eyes darting between them. "Home or vacation?"

Lily chanced a glance at Ford, wondering if he too was wrestling with the urge to explain that they weren't actually traveling together, that it was just a random twist of fate that had the two of them sharing the same air, heading towards the same final destination.

Ford, for his part, seemed to be feeling no such need to clarify. "Wellington," he said with a smile. "And it's home. How about you?"

Only when he said it did she realize it was true. Though it had felt like a joke or a half-truth, something the two of them would smile about later, it was her new reality. She wasn't going to Wellington for vacation, and while she wasn't returning there after any length of time away, it *was* going to be her new home.

"Nice," the man was saying. "Sydney is the final destination for me, thank goodness. If I don't see the inside of another airplane after this ever again, it'll be too soon."

Ford nodded. "I hear that, mate. Wish I could say the same was true for us, but at least it's just a short one from Sydney to Wellington. Should be home before we know it."

As the conversation between the two of them continued around her, Lily smiled along, all the while pondering Ford's words. She wasn't going home with him, she knew that much. She had an apartment waiting for her that the Weta Workshop had arranged on her behalf, and judging by the photos she had already seen online, she was going to love it. She wondered, though, where Ford lived. Were they in the same neighborhood? Within walking distance of each other? Would she be seeing him again in a day or two, or would it be at least a week before their paths crossed again?

There were still so many unknowns, and she was trying her hardest not to get caught up in them. They still had the rest of this flight ahead of them, not to mention the layover in Sydney and another flight after that.

Still, it was just like Lily to get caught up in the logistics of things. She didn't have a prearranged ride from the airport, had politely turned down her new supervisor's offer to pick her up, uninterested as she was in making the sort of first impression that could only be made after a full day of uncomfortable travel. She had the address of her new home and a basic understanding of her options for getting there, knowing she could either take a taxi from the airport or brave public transportation if she was feeling alert enough to do so.

How was Ford going to get home? Had he arranged for someone to pick him up? Maybe the two of them could share a taxi.

She was beginning to spiral, getting swept up in the uncertainties of what awaited her in Wellington when Ford got her attention with a gentle caress of her shoulder.

"Hey," he said, his eyes searching hers. "What's going on in that mind of yours?"

It was as if he could sense the chaos of her mental chatter without her even needing to say a word.

"Nothing," she said, taking his hand in her own. "Or nothing that can't wait until we land in Wellington, at least."

Seven

The remainder of the flight—up to and including the landing, Lily was pleased to report—went off without a hitch. Ford gripped her hand as they approached the runway, but apart from a slight bounce as they touched down, it was nothing but smooth sailing. She squeezed his hand as they slowed to a drivable speed, following a series of turns as they made their way to the gate.

"We made it," she told him, taking her hand back. "Feels good to be on the ground again."

Ford nodded fervently. "It might be the wrong country, but it's one giant step closer to home, so I'll take it."

They made their way off the plane, following the signs for international transit passengers and going through a security check, and it wasn't long before they found themselves approaching their new gate, their temporary home, while they waited to depart for Wellington.

"So, this is it," said Ford, gesturing towards the gate. "Now that we've seen it, shall we show ourselves around a bit, see what else Sydney's finest has to offer?"

"Sure," she replied. "It would be a good idea to stretch our legs a bit, but apart from that, I don't have much else on my radar."

"Maybe a coffee?" he asked, wiping his bleary eyes. "It's no substitute for sleep, but it's at least a better idea than a beer."

"Oof," she said with a wince. "I know all bets are off in the airport and time zones aren't real, but beer sounds like the furthest thing from a good idea. Water. We need water, and lots of it."

"You've got it. Water and coffee, in that order. Come on." They maneuvered their way to a nearby cafe, where Ford insisted on treating Lily to "her first southern hemisphere water and coffee."

"Besides," he said. "It's not like you have any Australian dollars on you, is it?" He reached over to tap his credit card on the reader as he quirked an eyebrow in her direction, and she barked out a laugh.

"It's not like you have any either," she said, nodding towards the credit card. "But I do appreciate it." They took their drinks with them, sipping and chatting as they made their way around the terminal. They paused in front of a "Welcome to Sydney" sign to snap a selfie, with Lily leaning her head against his shoulder, sure her face was the picture of delirious, blissful exhaustion.

"Okay, that's enough walking," she said, a hand landing on his forearm to tug him towards the gate. "I'm too tired to keep standing up."

Ford looped an arm through hers and directed her back to the gate, finding a seat for her with an empty one next to it, where he left his bag. "Can you give me your boarding pass, so I can go see if I can get our seats changed?"

She had forgotten all about that, forgotten that he wasn't already a fixture in her life. "Sure," she said, fishing it out of her bag. "Do I need to come with you, so they know this is a real request and that you aren't a creep who pickpocketed me and is now trying to sit next to me?"

He frowned. "That does sound like an unlikely scenario, but maybe just keep an eye on me up there at the counter. If I turn and give you the nod, then you can just give a wave and a thumbs up, so they know you're in on this whole scheme of mine. I'll only ask you to come up there as an absolute last resort since, by the looks of it, you can barely keep those eyelids open."

"Thank you," she said, giving him a smile that she was sure read at least as much sleep-dumb as it did appreciative. "You're the best."

An hour later, they were boarding their final flight, newly assigned seats right next to each other in the emergency exit row.

"Only for you," Ford had told her, "would I agree to sit in the emergency exit row. It was that or sit in aisle seats across from each other, and that didn't exactly seem conducive to conversation—or to making our neighbors not hate us."

"You don't like the exit row?" She leaned towards him as they settled into their seats, her voice once again only for him. "I'd think you'd want to have prime access to the exit in case of, you know, an emergency—"

"I'm going to stop you right there," he cut in. "No reminder needed of just exactly what the intended purpose of this row is. No, if you must know, my objection to it is about the responsibility of it all. I've never actually sat in it before, but I've sat just behind—those are the best seats in the house, by the way—and heard the spiel they give them up here. Apparently, once the people in this row open up the door—" He shuddered at the thought. "—they then have to man it while everyone else exits the plane. They're right there, able to see their freedom, but they can't partake of it until everyone else is out of harm's way."

Lily gave him a pat on the knee. "Well, I do appreciate you taking this particular chance on my behalf. And I'm sure it won't help, but if I can remind you that it's incredibly unlikely we'll need to do anything even remotely related to emergency exit tasks today—"

He held up a hand, and she stopped speaking, smiling at him as he reached for the information card in front of him. "You know it doesn't help, so I'll save you the effort then." He looked between the diagrams on the card in front of him and the door next to her, for Lily had taken the window seat on this particular flight. Ford pointed at one of the early boxes on the diagram, then reached towards the handle at the top of the emergency exit door.

"What are you doing?" Lily asked, her hand coming up to enclose his. "I don't know much about emergency exit row responsibilities, but I'm pretty sure you definitely aren't supposed to take a test run on opening up the emergency exit."

"I wasn't going to," he said, goggling at her like she was the one doing something completely absurd. "I was just familiarizing myself with where everything is. Though, if you ask me, it does seem ridiculous that we're given all this responsibility and then don't even get to take it on a test run."

"Does it really?" She cocked her head at him. "Because I'm pretty sure emergency exits don't just open and shut like regular doors. If they had you test that out now, there's probably some special procedure to seal it back up, and that would add hours to our journey."

"And that's the last thing anyone wants," he agreed, looking at the door wistfully. "Still, it would be great if there was like a weekend class or something, where you could practice the whole emergency exit procedure and then get, like, a certificate that lets you sit in this row."

He stretched out his legs in front of him, sighing with pleasure when his knees didn't touch the seat in front of him. "I can see why people like this row, though. Even if the responsibility that comes with it is the stuff of my actual nightmares."

"It's okay, Ford," she said, moving their hands together to the armrest. It was clear their seat choice had kicked his flight anxiety into high gear, and they weren't even pushing back from the gate yet. "I'll be right here with you, and we'll be home before you even know it."

He smiled at her. "I like that you called it home. I know you did it for my benefit, and I'm sure Wellington doesn't feel remotely like home to you yet, but...you're going to love it."

She hoped so. Hoped the city was full of people as kind as Ford, and that she'd find a community of friends to be her second family. Hoped the scenery—and those weekend excursions with Ford—were as full of beauty as all the photos she'd seen online. Hoped the homesickness she had felt over the last day would be a distant memory and that her new life would be full of joy.

"I think I will," she told him. "And if it isn't love at first sight, I'll do my best to make it work. Maybe Wellington and I can go to couple's therapy together, if it comes down to it."

He shook his head, but he was smiling at her. "That won't be necessary. I'll make sure she's on her very best behavior for you, that she makes the right sort of first impression. And then if you ever need anything, I'll be just a phone call away."

"Yeah?" she asked, unable to keep the hope out of her voice.

"Definitely. You won't be getting rid of me anytime soon, Lily." He squeezed her hand back. "Unless you want to, of course. I'm not going to force myself into your life if you want nothing to do with me."

"Good to know," she told him, "but it's not going to happen. Not only would it not make even the tiniest bit of sense to scare off the only person I know in Wellington—or New Zealand as a whole, for that matter—but I actually really like having you around. So far, at least." She gave him a nudge in the ribs. "It'll be fun," she said, "spending all that time together. I'm pretty sure this day of travel has bonded us for life."

Again with the coming on too strong, she chided herself. *Just because this man still wanted to spend time with her, that didn't mean he wanted to be tethered to her for the rest of his time on this mortal coil.*

But before she could backtrack, dial down the intensity of her words, he reached an arm around her shoulder and pulled her close, dropping a very unexpected kiss on the side of her head. "Funny how that happened, isn't it?"

The flight to Wellington was a short one, only three hours long. The takeoff had gone smoothly, with Ford's hand in hers, his eyes gripped tightly shut when the flight attendant had asked them to agree to the responsibility of sitting in the exit row seat. He had nodded vigorously, as if doing so would keep her from saying the things he so desperately didn't want to hear.

And just like that, sooner than they had realized, they were in the air, leaving Australia behind as they made their way to New Zealand. The flight wasn't long enough for entertainment to be a concern, so Ford and Lily had passed the time making conversation and playing I Spy out the window. After a few rounds of the game, where each of them had spied the ocean and a cloud in turn, they had shifted it into the realm of the imaginary, their focus shifting to creatures of the deep. They had spied a megalodon, a kraken, and even the Loch Ness Monster, a very long way away from home.

When the first hints of land became visible, New Zealand drawing into view, the pilot came on to make an announcement. "Ladies and gentlemen," she said, "it looks like we're expecting Windy Wellington to live up to its name today, and that our landing might be a bit on the bumpy side. We're asking everyone to return to their seats, make sure their seatbelts are tightly fastened, and prepare for landing."

Lily looked at Ford, his hand already in hers, and she gave it a squeeze. "It'll be fine," she said, and he nodded.

"Of course it will. It's the last bit of this whole journey. They can't take us down now, can they?"

She shook her head at him. "What are we even going to talk about when we remove jokes and suggestive comments about our relative safety in the air?"

He shrugged, but as the plane began to experience some turbulence, the color drained from his face. "We'll figure something out," he managed.

Lily kept her hands on Ford's, her eyes trained out the window, like she was the one landing the plane. She could see the land approaching, the plane dipping and weaving.

That was a new experience. After the day they'd had, she was accustomed to the stomach-lurching drops of the turbulence experienced high above the earth. But the closer they came to land—and she hoped to a runway because she couldn't see it from her window—the more the plane dipped, not just down, but side to side.

After one particularly gusting wind and a sharp lurch to the side, she felt her stomach drop as she gripped Ford's hands so tightly she expected her nails to leave marks.

This was it. They were going down. They had to be.

It looked like they were about to slam sideways into the land. She was so sure they had misjudged where the airport was. Still, there was no runway that she could see, only the shore and the land and the crashing waves marking the line between them.

And then just as she was about to scream something at Ford about how he was right, how air travel was the worst, the most dangerous, how this was the end, she felt the plane touch down on the ground beneath them. The brakes engaged, and they began to slow.

For the first time in her life, she forced her hands together, clapping with her mouth agape and overcome with relief. The sound of her own blood rushing in her ears was so loud, she didn't even know if anyone else was clapping. Not until she looked at Ford and saw him doing the same.

She blew out a sigh. "That was intense."

He nodded. "It was probably the worst part of the whole journey."

"Yeah, definitely." She nodded. "As if I wasn't already relieved enough to be here. Now I'm not even sure if I ever want to leave."

The color was returning to his face, and a smile graced it now, too. "I see no reason why you should," he told her.

Just before they parted ways at passport control, they made plans to meet at the baggage claim. Lily was greeted by a smiling passport control agent who looked over her passport and the visa inside that authorized her to stay and work. She welcomed her to Aotearoa and sent her on her way.

Before Lily could even find a screen to check which baggage carousel to look for, she found Ford slipping into place beside her, an arm around her shoulders, steering her in the right direction.

"You did it," he said. "You made it. You're here. They let you in. And now you're not going anywhere."

She smiled up at him, all the tiredness of the day catching up with her. "Well, I hope I'm going to my new apartment," she said. "At some point, I mean. I'm not sure I've ever been this tired in my life."

He nodded as he grinned back at her. "Of course. I was meaning to ask you," he said, "if you needed a ride home."

Before she could even think of what the polite response would be, she found herself nodding. "I would love that," she said. "I would *really* love that."

Eight

Outside the airport, Lily took a moment to stop and breathe, taking in her surroundings. The air was warm, a welcome reminder that while it was the middle of fall back home in Wisconsin, now she was enjoying a spring breeze with summer just around the corner.

"I can't believe this is really happening," she told Ford, who had stopped near her and was just watching her, an expression on his face that she couldn't totally make sense of. "There's so much that I want to see and do and experience…" She trailed off, shaking her head at herself. "But I want to do all of that tomorrow. Today…today I'm just too tired for any of it. I want to sleep for 13 hours at least, and then I want to start over again on my first impression I'm making on New Zealand."

"Not necessary," he said. "The first impression, I mean. New Zealand already adores you. And there would be something wrong with it if it judged you for your basic human needs." He held out a hand to her. "Come on. I'll take you home, and we'll get you settled there."

It was a short drive from the airport to Lily's new home, and Ford was like a different person behind the wheel of his familiar car. Gone were the anxiety and nerves, replaced by a self-assured, alert driver with no evidence of the fatigue he must have surely been feeling.

On the way from the airport to her apartment, they drove by houses built on steep cliffs, a variety of steep stairs and private cable cars helping those residents carry themselves and their groceries up to their homes. They drove by the harbor, and Lily took it all in, too tired even to make mental notes of what she wanted to check out in more detail the next day.

When Ford parked the car in front of her new home, she felt a twinge of nerves. She wanted to ask him to come in with her, wanted someone to be with her when she saw her new home for the first time, but she didn't want to imply that she meant anything more than that. Not now. Not this soon after meeting each other, and certainly not after the world's longest day of travel.

But he was already opening his door. "Come on, I'll carry your bag up for you. If you don't mind, that is, I'd like to see this place they've got you in. Make sure it's up to the standards you deserve." He gave her a wink, and she nodded, falling in to step beside him.

They found their way to Lily's new apartment, the instructions she had received via email taking at least twice as long to decode in her sleep-deprived state. The key had been left in a lockbox, and unlocking the thing had taken her right back to the days she had first been assigned a locker in middle school, turning that dial to the right and left and messing it all up on at least every third attempt.

Inside, Ford let out a low whistle. "This is a great place," he said, nodding towards the view of the harbor out the living room window. He walked into the kitchen, opening the cupboards and refrigerator. He made a tsking sound, shaking his head. "This, however, won't do. You need sustenance, Lily. What's going to happen when you wake up from your 13-hour nap ready to eat the world and there's nothing here?"

She groaned, flopping onto the couch. "Is it terrible if I say that sounds like a problem for future me? I'm too exhausted to stand up, much less hobble along to the grocery store and hem and haw over which brand of cereal to buy."

He joined her, the couch dipping low with the weight of him next to her. "It's completely understandable," he said, pulling out his phone and busying himself on the screen.

"What are you doing?"

"Letting my sister know I've landed, but that I'm not going to be back home right away." He turned to look at her. "The next part is up to you."

She shook her head at him. "No idea what you're talking about."

"Well, considering that I've gotten a bit of a second wind and feel pretty good right now, I could either do a quick grocery shop for you…"

"Or?" she asked, frowning slightly at him. There was no way she was letting this man run her errands for her. Even if he felt fine at the moment, she knew he'd gotten just as little rest as she had and must surely be in desperate need of some solid sleep.

"Or I could crash on your couch and take you out for a proper meal when we both wake up." His cheeks had deepened in color as he patted the cushions, his eyes not meeting hers.

"Hmm, almost," she said, giving him a smile that he couldn't see, his attention still fixed on determining just how firm the couch cushions were. "How about we both get some sleep and then we order in?" She nodded towards the TV mounted on the wall. "You can introduce me to the best Kiwi channels and we can eat...well, it will be up to you to know what's good here. Thai food? Japanese?"

Ford's eyes had brightened since she had revealed her plan, and he was already nodding along. "That's perfect," he said, scooching to one end of the couch and kicking off his shoes. He nodded towards the hallway, towards her bedroom that lay there just out of sight. "Now you hurry up and get some rest, too, so the real fun can begin."

She shook her head at him. "This has got to be the weirdest first date I've ever been on."

"First date?" He gave her an incredulous look, and she felt a growing sense of discomfort. She had misread the situation. He wanted to be her friend, he had made a friendly offer, and now she was making it weird.

"The way I see it," he continued, "LA to Sydney counts as the first date, then we had a coffee date in the Sydney airport as our second date, and for our third date we thought we were going to crash into the sea." A dimple appeared as his full grin spread across his face. "This evening has fourth date written all over it."

"Well, okay then," she said, getting to her feet and beginning to shuffle towards her room. "So I'll see you in..."

"Twelve to thirteen hours," he replied, stretching out to his full height with his head on one of the couch's arms, his eyes already closing. "Looking forward to it."

"So am I," she said. "Pick me up at...whatever time that is, I guess."

"Will do. Wear something cute." She looked back to find him watching her, earning herself a wink in response. "I'm kidding about that. It's going to be a cozy evening. Leave the high heels in your suitcase."

"If you think I'm unpacking before our date, then you are deeply mistaken."

His eyes were closed again. "I'm hearing a lot of talking out of you still, Lily, when what I should be hearing is the sound of you sleeping. Off to bed with you, now."

She blew him a kiss before turning on her heel. "Sweet dreams," she called over her shoulder. "See you on the other side."

"Can't...wait..." he murmured, before slipping off into sleep.

Alone in her room, Lily couldn't stop smiling. Nothing had gone the way she expected it to, and yet it all felt so deeply right. "This is the beginning of something great," she whispered to her reflection in the mirror above her new dresser, before flopping directly on top of the blankets on her bed, sleep coming for her before her head even hit the pillow.

Author's Note

Thank you so much for joining me for Lily and Ford's story. I've enjoyed the airplane-based adventures of the "Catching Flights & Feelings" series so much, to the point where it actually makes me look forward to long flights and all the inspiration that can strike there.

If you haven't yet read the other books in this series (since they can all be read independently but are very loosely interconnected), be sure to check out *At Your Altitude* and *Frequent Flyers*.

To stay updated on other works in progress or purchase books and bundles directly from me, please visit my website at kcmccormickciftci.com.

If you loved this book, please consider leaving a review, as that is one of the best ways to support indie authors like me. Reviews left on major retail sites (wherever you bought this book is a great start!), Goodreads, and Book-Bub will help other readers discover this book, too.

About the Author

KC McCormick Çiftçi is an English teacher turned romance writer. She spent the majority of her twenties living and working abroad, collecting the experiences that inform the stories she tells. She enjoys telling multicultural and international love stories through romantic comedy and women's fiction. She lives in Turkey with her husband and a herd of cats.

Prior to diving into the world of romance, KC published two self-help books for intercultural couples, *Loving Across Borders* and *The K-1 Visa Wedding Plan*. Both are available wherever books are sold.

For updates on upcoming releases, behind the scenes news, and all my favorite book recommendations, visit kcmccormickciftci.com (or just point your phone camera at the QR code below).

Books by KC McCormick Çiftçi

Austen in Turkey
Pride, Prejudice, & Turkish Delight
Sense, Sensibility, & the Mediterranean Sea

Home (Abroad) for the Holidays
Christmas on Inishmore
Christmas at Terminal One
Christmas by the Sea

Intoxicated by You
Intoxicated by You

Cats of Istanbul
The Vet Upstairs
From Strays to Soulmates
Whiskers and Wanderlust

Choose Your Own Adventure
We Were Inevitable

Intercultural Relationship Self Help

Loving Across Borders
The K-1 Visa Wedding Plan